The
Christmas
Kitten

Written by ANDREW CHARMAN

Illustrated by JOHN BLACKMAN

Derrydale Books
New York/Avenel, New Jersey

A TEMPLAR BOOK

This 1992 edition published by Derrydale Books,
distributed by Outlet Book Company, Inc., a Random House Company,
40 Engelhard Avenue, Avenel, New Jersey 07001.

First published in Canada in 1992 by Smithbooks,
113 Merton Street, Toronto, Canada M45 1AB.

Devised and produced by The Templar Company plc,
Pippbrook Mill, London Road, Dorking, Surrey RH4 1JE, Great Britain.

Edited by A J Wood
Designed by Janie Louise Hunt
Printed and bound in Singapore

ISBN 0-517-06968-7
8 7 6 5 4 3 2 1

It was Christmas Eve and everyone in the animal shelter was having fun. They were glad to be inside in the warm and not outside in the cold city streets, fighting over scraps of food. It was bright and noisy in the shelter and full to overflowing with cats of all shapes and sizes. Some were neatly groomed and others were shabby, but mostly they were cats from the streets who had nowhere else to go.

Ginger, the biggest and bossiest of the cats, had organized a game of tag. Cats were running and jumping everywhere. Suddenly, one cat pushed another as he ran past. The other cat pushed back, and a fight started. Soon others joined in. They fell into a heap, claws flashing, hissing, scratching, and biting. Like a hurricane, the fight swept across the room, gathering everyone in its path.

In the corner was a little kitten who was trying not to be noticed. The fight engulfed him. A paw struck him in the face. The kitten heard a buzzing noise and the room spun. Then suddenly he felt as if he was flying. He just had time to see the other cats below him looking up in wonder before he hit the ground with a bump. Ginger had pulled him out by his tail.

"You're going to have to keep your wits about you if you're going to survive in this place," laughed Ginger. "What's your name, little one?"

"Oliver," replied the kitten, trembling.

"It's a tough life in the shelter, Oliver," said Ginger. "I can see that I'm going to have to give you a few tips on self-defense. Now, what do you do if a cat comes up behind you without warning?"

"Run?" suggested Oliver.

"No, you spin and slash," laughed Ginger. "Don't give them time to think." Ginger suddenly spun around and lashed out with his paws. His gleaming claws sank into the wall, leaving a row of deep scratches. "That's the way," he said, proudly.

"But I thought cats were supposed to live with families," said Oliver, surprised. "They sleep in front of the fire and lap up bowls of milk and have plenty of time for grooming."

"You're in the wrong place if that's what you want," laughed Ginger. "Around here we turn kittens into street-fighting tigers." And with that the big cat strolled off, muttering to himself.

Oliver washed his paw thoughtfully, and
wondered at what Ginger had said. He had only been
in the shelter for a couple of weeks and he couldn't
remember very much about where he'd been before
that. But he guessed he must have been with a "family,"
whatever that was, and that was how he knew about
them. He certainly didn't like the idea of becoming a
street-fighting tiger.

"Perhaps I am in the wrong place, then,"
thought Oliver to himself. Small and weak though he
was, Oliver was strong in his mind. He knew what he
wanted. He wanted to be in a family, and he was
going to find one. He decided to escape.

Later, when the food arrived, Oliver saw his chance. As the others crowded around the bowls of food, he crept quietly out of the partly-opened door. He scampered quickly down the bright corridor and through another door. He was inside a cupboard. Then, just when he thought he'd have to go back and find another way out, he saw it. A hole. What luck! It was just large enough for Oliver to squeeze through.

In no time at all, he was running along a narrow tunnel. He could feel a draught of cold air whistling through his whiskers. The outside couldn't be far.

Oliver heard voices ahead and suddenly the tunnel opened out into a large underground cave. He could see movement below him. As his eyes became accustomed to the dim light, Oliver saw hundreds of small, furry animals. They had sleek gray fur, long pink tails, and twitching whiskers. They were mice!

"Can we begin?" said a large mouse who had climbed onto an empty can in the center of the throng. "I have called the family together to discuss an important issue." Oliver's ears pricked up at the sound of the word "family".

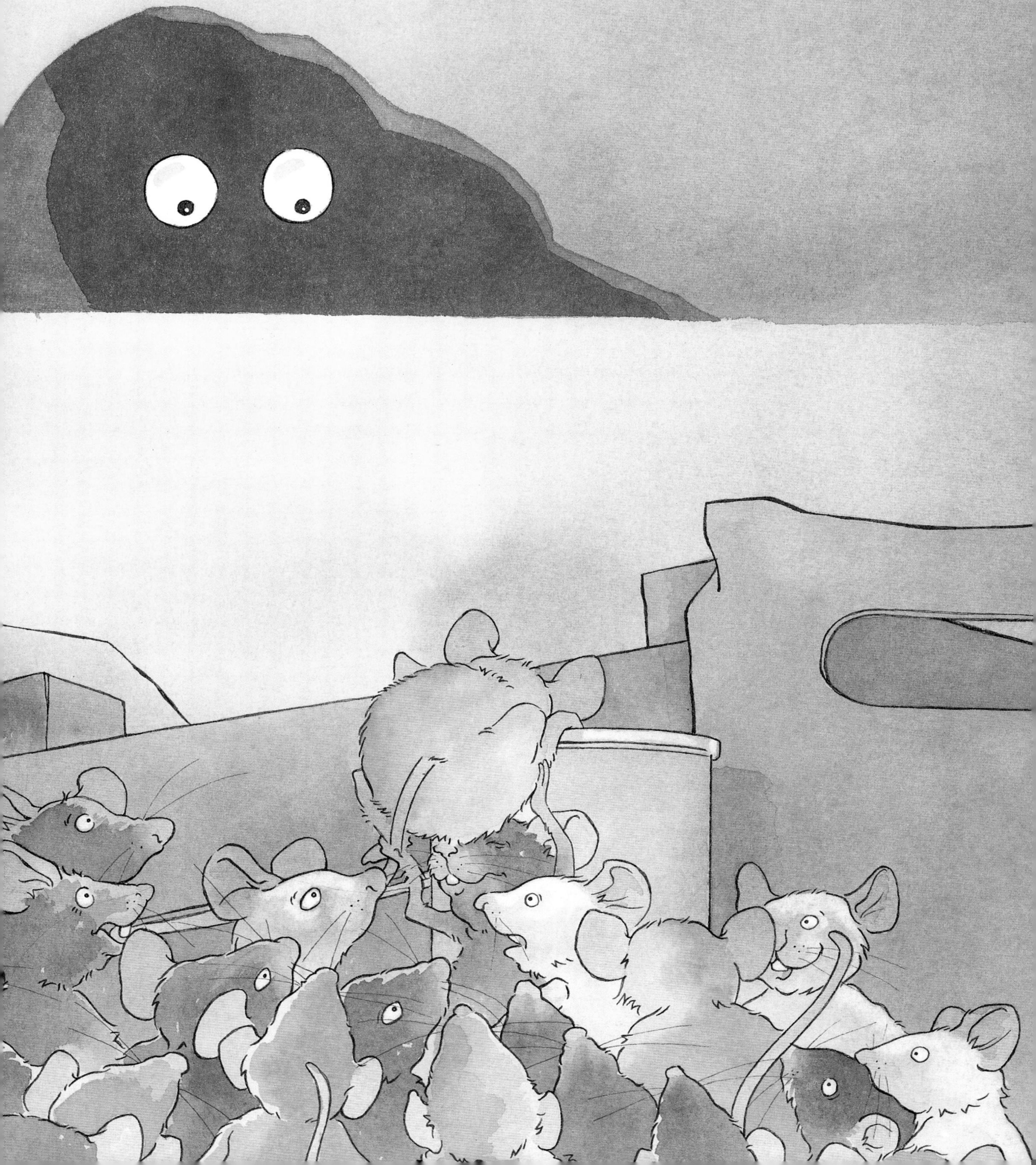

"Now as you all know," the big mouse went on, "tomorrow is Christmas Day and we have planned our usual family celebration…" But he didn't get a chance to continue for Oliver could not hold himself back any longer. He jumped down from the ledge, shouting eagerly:

"Can I join your family? Oh, please let me join."

Chaos immediately broke out all around him.
Mice fled in every direction. Oliver heard shouts of
"Quick, cats!" and "Run for your whiskers!" as the mice
climbed over each other to get away. Seconds later,
the underground cave was empty. Poor Oliver couldn't
understand it.

"Whatever did I say!" he thought to himself.
"Anyway, that's obviously not the right kind of family
for me." So he shrugged his shoulders and walked on.

Soon Oliver reached the open air. An icy wind was blowing through the streets, and it had started to snow. Large flakes fell onto his fur and melted. Before long he was wet and bedraggled. The city looked strange and frightening. Lights flashed and cars roared past. Oliver trudged along the sidewalk, feeling unhappier than he had ever felt.

Then Oliver heard an unfamiliar sound. He'd never heard it before, but he knew just what it was all

the same. "WOOF!" it went again. He turned and there it was, a little way off, but getting closer – ears flapping, mouth dribbling, huge wet paws slapping against the ground. A dog! An enormous, hairy dog was bounding toward him.

One of the cats at the shelter had once told Oliver that dogs were harmless and that they just wanted to play. But Oliver wasn't about to stay and discover if that was true.

Oliver took one look at the dog's wet, wobbling mouth, and fled. For an instant, he was running on the spot, slipping on the icy ground. Then he shot forward, running as fast as he could.

Oliver rounded a corner and glanced behind him. The dog was getting closer. Just then, a taxi stopped ahead of him. A woman who had been standing beside the road opened the door. Oliver didn't have time to think. He jumped straight into the open taxi and dived under a seat. The door slammed shut.

The dog skidded, spun around twice before stopping, and barked as he watched the taxi drive away through the snow. Oliver crouched under the seat and listened to his heart beating.

"Phew!" he thought. "That was close."

Oliver lay very still. Neither the driver nor the passenger had seen him. They were busy talking about Christmas Day, just like the mice.

"I promised her one for Christmas," the woman was saying. "But all they had at the pet shop were rabbits and guinea pigs…"

No, they definitely hadn't seen him. The air in the taxi was warm and the vibration of the engine soothing. Soon Oliver was fast asleep.

He awoke just in time to see the woman opening the door. Out he jumped, scurrying quickly away into the bushes at the side of the road.

Oliver looked around him. He was on the edge of a wood. Tall trees stretched up toward the sun, their branches weighed down with the snow that

had fallen only an hour before. It didn't look like the sort of place where you might find a family, but Oliver set off to search for one anyway. He struggled with difficulty through the thick snow. Sometimes he sank completely in drifts that came over his ears. Eventually, he came to a hillock which, for some reason, wasn't covered with snow. He scrambled to the top to see where he was. Suddenly, the hillock moved. It rose from the ground, swayed slightly, and yawned.

The hillock wasn't a hillock at all – it was a huge brown bear and Oliver was standing on it!

"I'm terribly sorry," said Oliver, nervously. "I thought you were a hill. I'll get down now and I won't bother you again."

"Oh, don't mind me," said the bear, yawning. "I didn't even notice you. I must have fallen asleep."

"Well, thank you," said Oliver climbing down carefully. "Actually, I came out here to look for a family, but now I think I'm lost."

"Well, you're not lost now. I've found you," said the bear, kindly. "But I don't know where you'll find a family around here. You can come and meet *my* family if you like. We're just getting ready for Christmas."

Oliver said he would love to meet a bear family so the two animals walked on together through the sunshine. Soon they came to a big cave in the side of a hill.

"This is where we live," said the bear. "You're lucky to find us up. We usually sleep at this time of the year because of the cold."

Then the bear introduced Oliver to his mother and father and all his brothers and sisters, and they all sat down for something to eat. There were berries and grasses, funny-looking grubs, and bowls of honey, but no saucers of milk. Oliver decided that he wasn't very hungry.

After the meal, the bears rolled in the snow to clean their fur and started yawning noisily.

"Time for bed, I think," said the first bear. "Are you coming, little animal?"

But Oliver had decided that a bear family was not the right sort of family for him. It appeared that they did not have fires *or* bowls of milk, and he really didn't like the idea of rolling in the snow to get clean. So he thanked them for their kindness and told them politely that he would continue on his way.

The bears waved Oliver goodbye and he promised that he would return to visit them in the spring when they would all be feeling more lively.

The sun was hanging low in the sky as Oliver set off once more through the trees. Every now and then, a tree would shiver in the wind and send a cascade of flakes to the ground.

Everywhere Oliver looked he could see

footprints in the snow. Oliver tried to follow them, but he wasn't sure in which direction they were going. He went around in circles several times before reaching the other side of the woods.

Listening hard, Oliver could hear unfamiliar noises – animal noises that he had not heard before. He climbed a tall bank and peered cautiously over.

On the other side was the biggest animal Oliver had ever seen. It had huge sturdy legs that looked like tree trunks, large flapping ears, and an impossibly long nose. The strange animal was eating bundles of hay.

"Hello," said Oliver, bravely.

"And how are you this fine festive season?" said the animal in an important voice. "Would you like some supper? I have an apple here somewhere that I was saving for just such a visit."

The animal stepped back to rummage in the hay. There was a loud crunch.

"Oh, bother," said the animal, lifting its foot from the squashed apple.

"Actually, I wasn't looking for food," said Oliver. "I am looking for a family. Do you know where I can find one?"

"Well, we all belong to the same family really," replied the animal thoughtfully. "Each and every one of us belongs to the family of animals."

"Of course, we're not all the same," the animal continued. "Some of us are mammals, and others are reptiles or birds. Were you looking for any particular species? We've got most of them here. Take me for instance. I'm an Indian elephant. That's Mammalia, Proboscidea, *Elephas maximus*. What are you?"

"I'm a kitten," replied Oliver who was very confused and wished that he had a more important-sounding name.

"Come over here and let me have a closer look," said the elephant. "Yes, I see – four paws, fur, whiskers, long tail. Can you see in the dark?"

"Oh, yes," replied Oliver. "Very well!"

"In that case there can be no doubt about it," said the elephant. "You are a cat, a carnivore of the family Felidae. *Felis catus* to be precise. I would suggest that you continue your search for a family in the cat's enclosure. It's at the far end of the zoo."

Oliver thanked the elephant and hurried away. When he looked back at the huge animal, it was studying the squashed apple.

"Yes," Oliver heard the elephant say to itself. "Difficult things, flat apples. Now if I can just get my trunk underneath it, perhaps…"

Oliver scampered off through the zoo. He passed many strange and wonderful animals that he had never seen before. The chimps were throwing snowballs at each other. An owl winked a large, orange eye at him. Snakes curled around branches and flicked out their tongues as he passed. A giraffe peered down at him from a great height. He never realised that there were so many animal families to choose from.

Eventually, Oliver arrived at the cat's enclosure. He could hear a fierce growling coming from inside. But he went bravely up to the fence and peeped in all the same. Inside was a huge cat with a long, sleek body striped with orange, white, and black.

"Excuse me," said Oliver.

The cat turned slowly and looked at him. Then it padded silently towards him and stared unblinkingly through the fence.

"I'm a cat," said Oliver, trying not to be put off by the other cat's menacing look. "And I'd like to join your family. Can I come and live with you?"

The huge cat looked at Oliver and slowly raised its eyebrows.

"Can you come and live with *ME*?" it repeated.

"Do you know *who I am*?" Oliver had to admit that he hadn't the faintest idea.

"I am a tiger," said the tiger. "I am the biggest and fiercest cat in the whole world. I am royalty, I am."

There was a pause while the tiger looked Oliver up and down again, and then he growled: "SCRAM, PUSSYCAT!"

"So that's what a tiger looks like," thought Oliver, remembering his conversation with Ginger. "Well, I never wanted to be one of them anyway."

He went up to the next cage and peered nervously in. Inside there was another huge cat, this time with a long, shaggy mane.

"Good evening," said Oliver politely. "Do you have a family I could join?"

But to Oliver's dismay the big cat just laughed.

"Ha, ha, ha!" he snarled. "I am a lion, King of all the Cats. You're far too small and scrawny to be in my family."

Poor Oliver! He backed away from the fence quickly and sat down heavily in the cold snow.

"Nobody wants me," he sobbed to himself. He covered his face with his paws and started to cry. He was so unhappy, he almost wished he was back in the animal shelter.

Suddenly a noise came from overhead.

"Psst!" it went. Oliver looked up. "Psst!" he heard again. Then he saw a scrawny cat beckoning to him from the top of a bank.

"Hey, Kitten," said the cat in a rasping voice. "You don't want to bother him, not if you know what's good for you. I heard what you said about looking for a family, and you're in the wrong place. Come with me."

The wise old cat led Oliver away from the zoo. Oliver could tell by the cat's accent that he came from the city.

"What you need, kid," said the cat, "is a family

of *HUMANS*." Oliver looked at him with surprise. "Don't worry," continued the cat who's name was Tom. "I know just the ones. I'll take you to 'em."

Tom knew all the tricks, and he led Oliver to a road with a row of houses. The two cats stopped outside a small house. It looked perfect. There was even a bottle of milk outside the door. The cat jumped nimbly up into a tree and walked along a branch that reached out toward the door. He pushed the bell.

There was a pause, then Oliver heard the sound of footsteps behind the door, and it swung open. A small, dark-haired girl looked out.

"Look Mom! Look Dad! It's a kitten. Oh, isn't he lovely?" The girl rushed forward and swept Oliver into her arms. "He's come to stay with us for Christmas. He's a Christmas kitten – just what I've always wanted," she cried.

"Well I never!" said her mother, and Oliver was most surprised to see the woman from the taxi. He looked around for the other cat, but he had vanished. The little girl carried Oliver inside and put him on a rug beside the fire, and her mom brought him a big bowl of milk.

"Oh, can we keep him?" asked the girl, excitedly. "You said this family needs a cat!"

"Well, yes, of course. If he wants to stay,"
replied her father. Oliver smiled to himself.
"Of course I want to stay," he purred. "I've got
lots of grooming to catch up on."